Dear Parent:
Your child's love of reading starts here!

Every child learns to read in a different way and at his or her own speed. Some go back and forth between reading levels and read favorite books again and again. Others read through each level in order. You can help your young reader improve and become more confident by encouraging his or her own interests and abilities. From books your child reads with you to the first books he or she reads alone, there are I Can Read Books for every stage of reading:

SHARED READING
Basic language, word repetition, and whimsical illustrations, ideal for sharing with your emergent reader

BEGINNING READING
Short sentences, familiar words, and simple concepts for children eager to read on their own

READING WITH HELP
Engaging stories, longer sentences, and language play for developing readers

READING ALONE
Complex plots, challenging vocabulary, and high-interest topics for the independent reader

I Can Read Books have introduced children to the joy of reading since 1957. Featuring award-winning authors and illustrators and a fabulous cast of beloved characters, I Can Read Books set the standard for beginning readers.

A lifetime of discovery begins with the magical words "I Can Read!"

*Visit www.icanread.com for information
on enriching your child's reading experience.*

**Visit www.zonderkidz.com/icanread for more faith-based
I Can Read! titles from Zonderkidz.**

ZONDERKIDZ

I Can Read Meet Fiona the Hippo
Copyright © 2020 by Zondervan
Illustrations © 2020 by Zondervan

An **I Can Read Book**

Requests for information should be addressed to:
Zonderkidz, 3900 *Sparks Drive SE, Grand Rapids, Michigan 49546*

Content contributors: Jesse Doogan and Mary Hassinger
Art direction and design: Cindy Davis

Printed in China

20 21 22 23 24 25 /DSC/ 15 14 13 12 11 10 9 8 7 6 5 4 3 2 1

ZONDERkidz · BEGINNING READING 1 · I Can Read!

Meet Fiona the Hippo

New York Times Bestselling Illustrator
Richard Cowdrey
with Donald Wu

ZONDERkidz

Meet Fiona.

She is a hippo.

That is short for the word

hippopotamus.

Fiona lives at
the Cincinnati Zoo.

When Fiona was born,

she was so tiny.

Fiona weighed 29 pounds!

That is very small for a baby hippo.

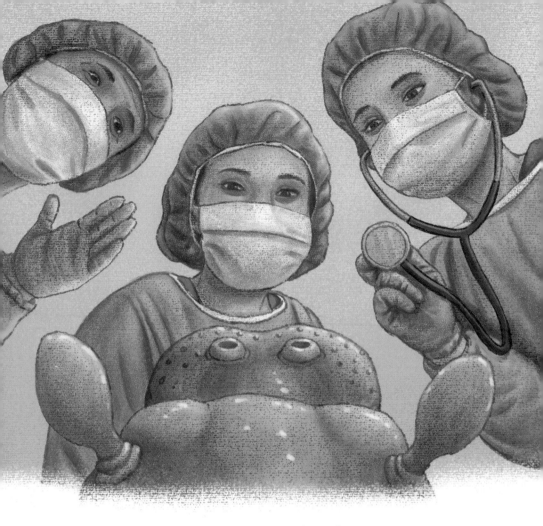

Many people helped Fiona
grow strong.
Doctors, nurses, and zookeepers
all helped. This group is called
Team Fiona!

Just like other babies,
Fiona had to drink milk from a bottle.

As Fiona grew bigger,
she liked to eat other food.

Fiona loved to eat lettuce!
She also loved to eat pumpkin,
watermelon, and pineapple.

Fiona had to learn how to walk.
Her helpers watched her as she tried
again and again.

"You've got this, Fiona!"
people would cheer,
as she took baby steps
around the room.

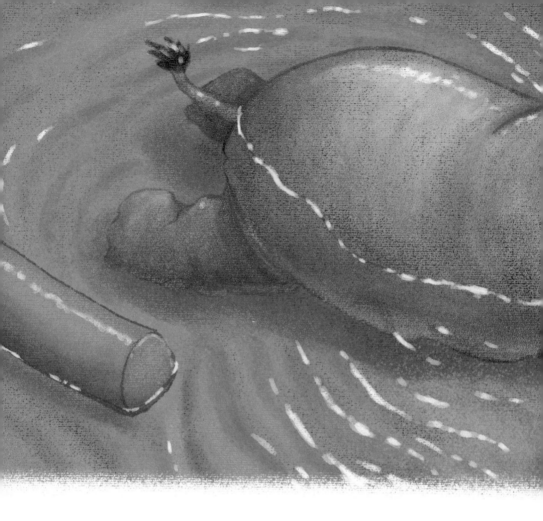

When Fiona was strong enough,
Team Fiona helped her learn to float.
Fiona had her very own pool.
She had her very own pool
noodles too.

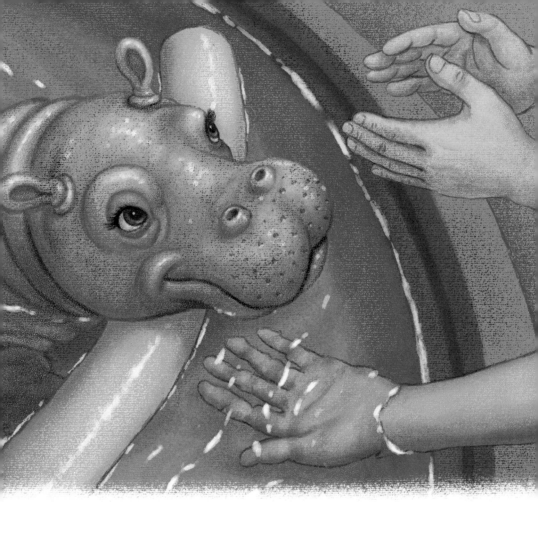

"You've got this, Fiona!"
people would cheer.
She loved to float
in the nice warm water.

Team Fiona taught her how to move
in her little blue pool.
Fiona learned fast!

Soon she could move and play
in the huge pool.
Fiona looked so small when
she was with her mommy and daddy.

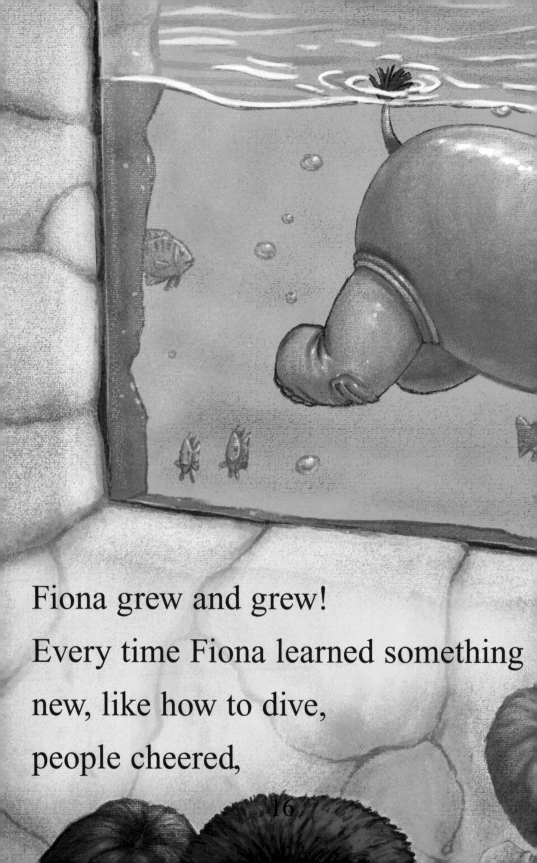

Fiona grew and grew!
Every time Fiona learned something
new, like how to dive,
people cheered,

"You've got this, Fiona!"
And she did!

Now, Fiona loves to play
in the water with the little fish
and with her very big mama.

Fiona looks out the window
of their pool.
She looks like she is smiling!

She loves to roll, dive,
and chase her mama
in the water.

Sometimes Fiona and her mama
just take naps in the water too.

People came from near and
far to the zoo
when Fiona was a baby.
They all wanted to see
the little hippo.

Everyone loved to see Fiona
wiggle her ears, snort, and play.
Soon, Fiona was famous!

Fiona got lots and lots of mail
from people called fans.

Fans are people who love
and support
Fiona and want her to
keep growing.

Now, Fiona is very healthy.

She is getting bigger and stronger.

Team Fiona is happy.

They watch her as she …

plays in the water

and eats good food.

Hippos like Fiona grow up
to be very big.
Someday Fiona might weigh more
than your family car!

And Fiona will have a huge mouth.
She will also have very big
teeth and tusks, just like her mama.

Even when Fiona is all grown up people from all over the world will still love her.

And the people will cheer,
"You've got this, Fiona!"

Five Hippo Facts

1. Hippos are mammals.
2. Hippos spend most of the day in the water.
3. Hippos can hold their breath for 5 minutes under water.
4. Hippos live in groups called bloats.
5. A baby hippo is called a calf.